FELICIA AND MIMI

Felicia & Mimi

written
&
illustrated
by
mel dietmeier

addison-wesley

An Addisonian Press Book

Felicia and Mimi live
with a cat named Noodle
in a little house
under a large bush
in the woods.

One morning Mimi was making a breakfast
of plums and shortbread cookies with currants.
She noticed that Felicia wasn't there.

Mimi immediately looked in the honey pot.
(Felicia was very fond of honey.)
But Felicia wasn't there.
And Mimi looked through all the spices . . .

. . . and she looked through
the canned stuff and the breads
and the silverware and the dishes
and the miscellaneous.
And Felicia wasn't there.
She wasn't even under the plums.

And Mimi looked in the teapot . . .
. . . and in the stove . . .

. . . and under the bed.

But Felicia wasn't there.

She wasn't in her shoes . . .

. . . or in the books . . .

. . . or in the trunk.

And then Mimi asked Noodle,
"Have you seen Felicia?"
But Noodle just shrugged his shoulders.
Mimi would have asked the mouse,
but he was busy stuffing himself
on a cookie.

Mimi sat down and said,
"Whew, humph."

Then suddenly
there was a knock at the door.
Mimi hurried to open it.

And there stood an unusual lady
wearing an extraordinary hat
with feathers and flowers stuck in it.
Mimi said, "May I help you?"
"Yes!" said the unusual lady,
"I am looking for Felicia."
"Oh!" said Mimi, "Why so am I.
And I can't seem to find her anywhere."

"Well," said the unusual lady,
"in that case
I shall look in my bag.
Perhaps she is there."
And she proceeded to remove
from her bag . . .

four round pebbles,

 a snail shell,

 one nickel,

 some stamps,

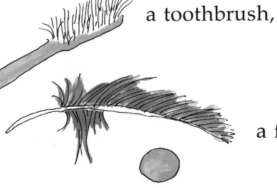 a toothbrush,

a feather,

 a plain marble
and
a striped marble,

 a peppermint flavored toothpick,

a string of safety pins,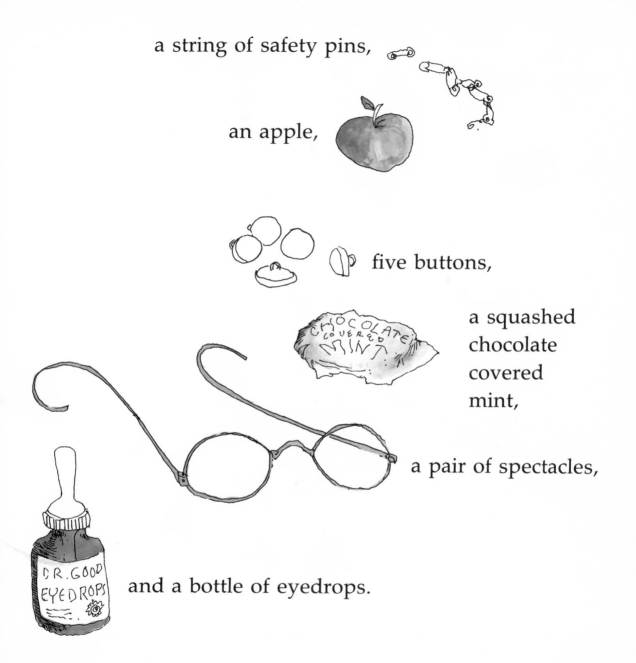

an apple,

five buttons,

a squashed
chocolate
covered
mint,

a pair of spectacles,

and a bottle of eyedrops.

"I keep all this with me just in case," she said.

Then her hat fell off.

And Mimi said,
"Oh, Felicia, you silly."
And Felicia said,
"Is breakfast ready?"

And so without further ado,
they sat down and ate.

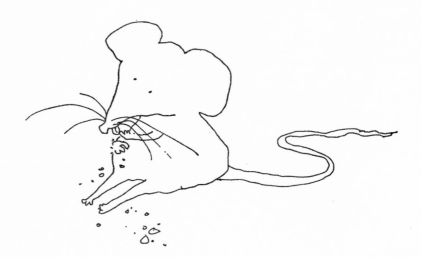